Blame It On
The Holidays

A Sugarplum Falls Bonus Epilogue Collection

Samantha Baca

Sugarplum Falls Series

Blame It On The Mistletoe

Blame It On The Eggnog

Blame It On The Candy Canes

Blame It On The Blizzard

Blame It On The Reindeer

Blame It On The Carols

Blame It On The Lattes

Blame It On The Secret Santa

Contents

Note From The Author

Thank you for coming back to Sugarplum Falls with me!

If you haven't read this series, you may want to go back and read the individual books before reading this, as it WILL have spoilers. This collection of bonus epilogues is intended to give updates on all of our favorite couples and where they are two years later.

It's also important to know that all of the original eight books were written in a way that didn't set a firm timeline of when each book happened in relation to the others. This was done on purpose so the books could be read in any order without any spoilers. The bonus epilogues contained in this book are continuations of their original stories.

In case you need a summary of who was in which book, I've added that information for quick reference below. Thank you for loving these characters and this series as much as I do!

Blame It On The Mistletoe—Jackson and Emily

Blame It On The Eggnog—Elliott and Sunny

Blame It On The Candy Canes—Zach and Andi

Blame It On The Blizzard—Sebastian and Brynlee

Blame It On The Reindeer—Brody and Jasmin

Blame It On The Carols—Aiden and Makayla

Blame It On The Lattes—Sam and Avery

Blame It On The Secret Santa—Sean and Cassidy

Blame It On The Mistletoe
One
Emily

"Look! It's Santa and Mrs. Claus!" I exclaimed, holding Jack's little hand up to wave as he watched the float go by.

"Do you think it's too cold for him?" Jackson asked, concern etched on his face.

"He's fine," I assured him with a laugh. "He's bundled in so many layers, he could pass as a cute little snowman."

"That would be thanks to the girls getting him ready in the car," Jackson replied, smiling as he looked over at Penelope, Gracelyn, and Sophie, who were sitting on the sidewalk, as far away from us as we would allow them to go. "They had fun picking which clothes he would wear today, but I swear they never agree on anything these days, so he's wearing a full outfit that each of them picked."

Having three preteen girls in the house was a struggle, and their recent quest for independence was a hard thing for me and Jackson to accept. Penelope pushed the hardest, but being the oldest meant that it was her job to test the waters. I constantly had to remind her that she was eleven, not twenty-one. Gracelyn and Sophie weren't as bad, but school had definitely changed them along with them watching their older sister grow up. But thankfully, the birth of their baby brother three months ago calmed a lot of it down, and the girls rallied around Jackson and me while taking care of the new baby of our family.

I shifted him in the carrier he was sitting in that was strapped to my chest and held both of his hands in the air as we waved at the kids and the rest of the floats that passed by. We weren't sure whether or not the girls would be interested in coming to the Frosty Fest parade this morning, but I was thankful that they didn't put up a fight over it because it was one tradition I wasn't ready to let go of.

Once the parade was over, Jackson took Jack—who he named, by the way—and went to the car to change him while I gathered the girls for a day of mommy-daughter shopping. I knew that Jackson would be close by if we needed him, but these moments were hard to come by, so I didn't want to waste any time.

"Where do you guys want to start?" I asked, looking around at all of the booths covering almost every open inch of space inside the mall. Frosty Fest was bigger than ever this year, with more vendors and way more out-of-town visitors.

"I need to get something for Nick," Penelope said, lowering her head as her cheeks flushed red.

My eyebrows rose as I wondered who this boy was and why she was getting him a gift.

"Who's Nick?" I asked.

"He's her *boyfriend*," Gracelyn teased, wiggling her eyebrows and making kissy faces.

I frowned and then turned my attention back to Penelope.

"I'm sorry—what?"

"It's not a big deal." She shrugged and stared at the linoleum floor instead of looking at me.

"You have a boyfriend, and it's *not* a big deal? I beg to differ."

"Can we please not do this?" she groaned, folding her arms over her chest and sighing heavily.

Ugh. The teen years were going to be just lovely.

"Do what?" I asked, throwing my hands up in confusion. "Ask about things going on in your life?"

"Embarrass me."

"Penelope, I'm not trying to embarrass you. But as your mother, I have a right to ask about this new boyfriend of yours. You're eleven. I didn't even say you could date yet."

"It's not like we're *going out* on dates or anything. Chill out."

"Who needs to chill out?" Jackson said, surprising me as he walked up and stood right behind me.

"Penelope has a boyfriend, and Mom is mad about it," Sophie explained.

"I didn't say I was mad about it," I objected, letting out a frustrated breath. "I just have questions that I would like answered."

"Me too," Jackson agreed. "Like, what's his name, and where does he live." His eyes narrowed as his brows furrowed.

I bit the inside of my cheek and tried not to laugh. I loved his overprotective side, even though the girls absolutely hated it.

"Dadddd," Penelope groaned, letting her head fall back.

"Nick," Gracelyn offered, a mischievous smile appearing.

"Does he go to your school?" Jackson questioned, his eyes narrowing further in deep concentration.

Jack started fussing, so I took him from Jackson as he continued to question Penelope. I walked over to an empty bench and sat down so I could feed Jack before getting the day started with the girls. Plus, I could already tell that I wasn't going to get anything out of Penelope right now. There was a slight chance she would open up and talk to Jackson about it, but if anything, at least he would put the fear of dating in her until I could get her alone later and have an honest discussion with her.

"Hey, sweetie," my mom said as she spotted me and came over to join me on the bench. "How's Jack liking his first Frosty Fest?"

"So far, he seems to like the reindeer. He kept trying to grab them in the parade. I think Jackson is going to take him to the pen in a bit to let him see them up close. But I don't know when we're going to try to do Santa photos. That line is insane, and the girls are less than patient these days."

My heart sank a little bit, knowing the fight they would put up before we got the family photos I desperately wanted.

"Yeah, I've never seen it this busy here before. It's like people got wind of Frosty Fest and came from all over the world to see it."

"Either that, or we got lucky to have two bestselling authors who are doing a book signing here. They've driven so much traffic to Sugarplum Falls that everyone is busy. I heard Andi say that she can't keep enough baked goods on the shelf before they sell out. Sam said that Sugarplum Lattes has had a line nonstop and that they have to have someone go outside and stand at the end of the line an *hour* before they close, just so they can get through everyone."

"Well, business is booming, and this town could definitely use it. I can only imagine how wonderful everyone's Christmas will be from all of this."

I nodded my head in agreement as Jack pulled away and started looking around. I covered myself before putting him up against my shoulder to burp him.

"Wanna go shopping with Nana?" my mother asked, holding her hands out to take him.

"You get him tonight," I said with a laugh. "Along with three possibly moody girls. You should go enjoy your alone adult time while you have it."

It was a long and busy day, with Frosty Fest happening during the day and the Mason, Inc. holiday party taking place tonight. I had tried to schedule the party for another night, but this was the only night that Sugarplum Suites had open when I booked everything for Mason, Inc. in September.

"Na. I don't need adult time," she replied, smacking her lips together to try to get him to smile. "I can actually take them with me when they're ready; that way, you and Jackson will have time to go home and get ready yourselves."

"It's just a company holiday party. I don't think we need to get all fancy, but thank you."

My mom squeezed my thigh gently to get my attention and smiled.

"You guys haven't had a night to yourselves in months. Get dressed up. Go have a few drinks. You guys have a room at the hotel the party is at so you don't have to worry about any adult responsibilities tonight. You owe it to yourselves to have a little fun for once."

I took a deep breath in and released it slowly. She was right. I couldn't remember the last time Jackson and I had any alone time together. It was probably the night Jack was finally conceived after trying for months without any luck. Then we had one time when the girls stayed the whole weekend with my mom, and we went at it like rabbits the entire time. A month later, I was staring at two pink lines on a positive pregnancy stick.

<u>Two</u>

Jackson

"I would like to thank you all for attending tonight. I've said it before, and I'll say it again. Mason, Inc. would not be as successful as it is without all of you. Cheers." I lifted my glass of champagne in the air, hating that I had to stand in front of everyone to give a speech. But as the CEO of the company, it was only right.

Everyone cheered, and glasses clinked around me. I took a sip and headed back to the table where Emily was waiting for me.

"Beautiful speech," she said, rubbing my thigh beneath the table. I reached down and captured her hand before she could go any further. While we were planning to stay here tonight, that didn't mean I could bail before dinner was served and go fuck her in our room the way I wanted to.

"Thank you." I leaned in and kissed her temple, not trusting myself to keep it PG-13 if I kissed her on the lips.

The waitstaff effortlessly moved about the room, delivering salads to each table. Our company had grown over the past few years, and thankfully, Emily stayed in charge of planning our holiday party. She also had the wise idea of booking a ballroom at Sugarplum Suites in September before everything sold out. Many of the employees took advantage of getting a room for the night with the discounted rate she scored for us. We also had a handful of new employees who worked remotely out of state and had come in for our last mandatory meeting of the year, which was also planned to coincide with the holiday party so they could attend both.

"Did you guys go to the Frosty Fest parade this morning?" Emily asked Paisley, one of our newer employees. She had been in town a few times before for meetings, but this was the first time she'd been to Sugarplums Falls during Christmas.

"We did! Julia loved it, but Wyatt wasn't as impressed," Paisley teased as her husband, Maverick, looked adoringly at her. "It feels weird to have a night without the twins, though. I'm still not used to it."

"It's hard," Emily agreed, nodding her head. "We got a room tonight, and all I can think about is what's going on with the kids and if they need me."

"Right? I've been the same way! Maverick keeps telling me not to worry and that they're fine, but I swear, I can't turn off that part of my brain."

"They're literally staying two rooms down from us with Callie and Dylan," Maverick replied, pressing a kiss to Paisley's hand. "Plus, they're having fun having a play date with Amelia. Trust me, we will hear if they need us."

I smiled, knowing what he meant from the few times Paisley was on a call with us for work, and the babies would suddenly start screaming in the background.

We chatted for a bit while I picked at my salad, not wanting to wait any longer to go up to the room and devour my wife.

A few hours later, dinner was done, a few drinks were had, and Emily and I danced until the friction on the dance floor became too much for either of us to bear. I practically dragged her out of the room, ready to throw her over my shoulder as she hiked up her floor-length dress to try to keep up with me.

Once we were in the room, I locked the door and pulled her into my arms. My lips crashed down over hers as her hands locked behind my neck. My hand slid up her side, grazing her breasts as I took my time touching every inch of her body.

She broke the kiss and stepped away, her eyes wild with desire. She turned around and pulled her hair to the side as she waited for me to unzip her dress. I slowly pulled the zipper down, taking my time before letting the fabric fall to the floor.

Emily looked ravishing wearing nothing but a black matching bra and panty set and black heels with thin straps that wrapped around her ankles.

I unbuttoned my dress shirt and tossed it to the floor, loving the way my wife's eyes lit up at the bulge my slacks failed to hide. She reached forward and gripped me tightly before undoing the button and unzipping them.

While I wanted to get right to making love to her, I also loved that we didn't have to rush tonight. For the first time in a long time, I didn't have to worry about anything else other than bringing pleasure to my wife and taking my time doing so.

Blame It On The Eggnog
<u>Three</u>
Sunny

"Did we get everything we came for?" I asked, staring at the bags piled underneath the double stroller that the twins were quickly outgrowing. It was like once they turned two, they went through a crazy growth spurt, and nothing fit them anymore. I had been kicking myself lately for not letting Elliott get the deluxe stroller that I had initially fallen in love with before the girls were born and convincing him that we didn't need something that extravagant when they would be home with me most of the time.

"That and then some," Elliott teased, smiling as the girls slept peacefully in the stroller, worn out from a full day at Frosty Fest.

"Dad, I'm hungry," Alex said, tugging on his hand.

"We still need to take our photos with Santa, so why don't we get a quick snack? Then we can go do our photos and head home," Elliott said, ruffling Alex's hair.

"Dadddd," Alex groaned, trying to pull away.

"Oh my gosh," I gasped, covering my face with my hands. "I completely forgot about the photos. Where is my head lately?"

"It's distracted with having twin toddlers that keep you on your toes, plus a son that just started kindergarten. Oh, and then there's the new baby on the way," Elliott teased, running a possessive hand over my swollen stomach.

"Yeah, because *someone* can't stop knocking me up."

"Hey, I gave it a few years before I got you pregnant again. If I had it my way, you would be knocked up all the time. Soon, we'll only be short a few kids for our own little league team."

"No, soon, we'll have to upgrade my car and get me one of those ugly, old lady vans for all of the kids I keep popping out."

"One—they're not ugly. Two—they're not old lady vans. We found a couple that looked more like an SUV, and you really liked them. Remember?"

"Yeah," I said with a heavy sigh, pushing the stroller toward the food court so we could get a snack for Alex as he walked beside me. "I also remember the price tag on them. The monthly payment on one of those would be more than what I was paying in rent for my apartment."

Elliott grabbed my arm and stopped me, already seeing the downward spiral I was heading into. I looked down to see Alex stop and check on his sisters.

"Did you forget what I do for a living?" he asked, pinching my chin between his fingers to bring my attention to him.

"I don't think the Cliterator 3000 is going to help us here," I whispered so Alex didn't hear me, scrunching my face. But I also wasn't about to judge said toy because it was by far the best thing Dark Vibes had ever made. I made sure to add one to my Christmas list this year, along with the Dark Horse.

"No." He pressed his lips together as a smirk played across them. "I mean, did you forget that I'm the CEO of a multibillion-dollar company and that money never has, nor never will, be an issue for us?"

"Elliott," I grumbled, trying to pull away. "I'm not going to just spend your money like that."

"It's not *my* money. It's *our* money, Sunny. You agreed to that when you married me. And I will not keep having these fights with you. Our family is growing, which means certain things in our lives will change accordingly. Now, you can either accept that and help me pick the vehicle you want, or I will buy what I think you'd like. Either way, you're getting a new ride."

"What if I don't want a new ride." I tipped my chin up defiantly, needing to get rid of some of this energy that was threatening to consume me. Being four months pregnant meant that I was constantly horny these days and thankful for Alex being in school so Elliott and I could sneak in quickies during the day since he worked from home.

Elliott's eyes darkened as he stepped closer and licked his lips.

"Trust me. You'll take it."

"And if I don't?" I pressed, feeling the heat of his body as he stood mere inches away.

"You will. You'll take it just like you take this cock every time I give it to you."

A shiver ran through me as heat flooded my cheeks. He stepped back and smirked again, this time not bothering to hide it as he put his hands on Alex's shoulders and guided him through the food court while I tried to get myself together.

<u>Four</u>

Elliott

"Do you know where we put the train set for Alex?" Sunny asked, bending over the pile of bags in the living room that we brought home from Frosty Fest.

"No, but we have time to find it," I promised, running my hand over her back.

"I want to try to get everything wrapped before he gets home. It's less than a week until Christmas, and there's a lot to get done."

"We have all night and most of tomorrow morning."

She stopped and stood up, tilting her head at me with a confused look on her face.

"What are you talking about?"

"I asked Beverly if she could take all three kids overnight. She said yes and will bring them back around eleven tomorrow morning."

"We have a kid-free night?"

I nodded, pulling my lower lip in between my teeth as Sunny's eyes widened before quickly turning into a frown.

"Stop it," she hissed, smacking my arm.

"Stop what?" I asked, laughing as I held my hands up.

"Stop looking at me like that. We might have a kid-free night, but I have a lot to get done, and I can't do any of it if you're balls deep inside me all night."

"I think some people would just call that multitasking," I teased, wiggling my eyebrows.

"Elliott," she scolded with a laugh.

I grabbed her arm and pulled her into me, needing her to stop obsessing over the mess of bags and gifts piled up in the living room.

"There's plenty of time to get all of this done, Sunny. But we have a rare gift of having uninterrupted time together. I don't want to waste it."

"Alright. I'll make you a deal," she said, placing her hands firmly on my chest. "You help me get all of this stuff wrapped and under the tree, and then we can spend the rest of the night doing whatever you want."

I knew that she wasn't going to be able to focus or disconnect from everything that was stressing her until we got through the pile in the living room.

"Deal," I said, extending my hand. She smiled and took it, not realizing the playful mood I was in, as I immediately lowered it to my cock that was already getting hard for her.

"Keep it in your pants," she warned, pulling away as she pointed a finger at me.

"You take all the fun out of it." I winked and moved the pile of stuff on the floor to the side so she didn't trip over it.

"No, the fun is what got me in this position to begin with," she teased, lifting the bottom of her shirt to show me her growing baby bump.

"You better stop," I warned, stepping beside her and yanking the fabric back down.

"Or what?"

"Or all of these gifts will go into gift bags so I can go fuck your brains out."

She rolled her eyes, knowing what it did to me, before plopping down onto the floor and pulling things out of the bags. I groaned dramatically as I grabbed the bag of wrapping supplies from the island and joined her.

Thankfully, we both worked fast and had the gifts wrapped and under the tree in record time. We had already done the majority of our shopping and still had a few bags of stuff hidden in the closet for when Santa came to visit. But these were the gifts that we saw and fell in love with today, which always happens during Frosty Fest. I didn't know a single person who lived in Sugarplum Falls who didn't wait until Frosty Fest to finish all of their shopping. There were always unique gifts that you were sure not to get anywhere else.

I helped Sunny get off the floor and then gathered the supplies and put them away. There were still a few bags full of stuff on the counter that we got from Frosty Fest but weren't presents.

"Oh no," Sunny said, pulling things out of the bag from Sugarplum Sweets with a frown on her face. "We didn't get any fudge or truffles."

"We still have time. I can run out later this week and pick some up."

"We need to get candy canes as well. Oh, and something for Alex to take for show and tell next week," Sunny added while scrunching her face. "I still can't believe he found my candy cane vibrator and wanted to take that."

"In all fairness, he thought it was some sort of Christmas present locator that vibrated when it found a present. He was excited to tell his friends about it."

"Thank goodness it hadn't been used yet. We need to find a better place for you to hide the new toys you bring home for us to try."

"Noted," I said with a chuckle as I picked up the sugar cookie decorating kit from the counter and raised an eyebrow.

"Those are for the kids to decorate cookies for Santa this year. I'm too tired to bake, and this comes with the pre-baked cookies and everything you need to decorate them. Andi is a genius for putting this set together." Sunny smiled softly.

I chewed my lower lip as I opened the box and started pulling the contents out.

"Elliott!" Sunny shrieked, rushing over to stop me. "Stop it! Those are for the kids!"

"I'll buy more," I said, my voice getting lower as dirty thoughts started to infiltrate my brain.

"She said she didn't think she would have more. I got one of the last sets. They've been flying off the shelves like hotcakes."

"Then I'll make cookies."

"*You're* going to make cookies?" she questioned with her

hand on her hip and an eyebrow raised.

"Sure. Why not."

I pulled out the bag of sugar cookies and set each one on the counter, looking for the Santa one I expected to be in there. What kind of set would it be if it didn't have a Santa cookie? A grin spread across my face when I spotted it and held it up for Sunny to see.

I set it down and then grabbed the tubes of frosting, looking to see which color I wanted. A few years ago, I had gone to a cookie decorating class with Sunny and Alex and found that I knew nothing about decorating cookies. The poor Santa cookie I attempted to decorate looked like Santa got a facial. Now I was going to purposely recreate that.

"What are you doing?" Sunny demanded, watching intently as I opened the white frosting and squirted a glob onto Santa's head.

"Just decorating some cookies like the old days."

"Like when you gave Santa a facial?"

"Yep. This time, I figured we could take it one step further, and I could give *you* one instead."

Her cheeks flushed with color, and her nipples puckered through the thin cotton t-shirt she was wearing without a bra.

"Well, two can play this game," she said, her sassiness coming out in full effect.

She grabbed the Mrs. Claus cookie from the counter and pulled out the barstool, making herself comfortable as she got the red frosting and opened it.

I watched with curiosity as Sunny worked, creating a red

bra and panty set on the cookie before opening a bag of sprinkles and picking two that she used as nipples.

My cock hardened, and I wasn't sure if it was because Sunny was making Mrs. Claus look like a smokin' hottie or if it was because she was taking this cookie decorating challenge to the next level and turning it X-rated.

I pulled out the other barstool and sat down, ready to play along. I grabbed a few sprinkles and placed them perfectly along the spot where Santa's dick would be if he had one, then covered it with red frosting, making sure the package was prominent.

While Sunny worked on creating a dirty Mrs. Claus, I worked quickly to frost my cookie, giving Santa an entire red outfit before using the black frosting pen and drawing Santa's arm and hand that went down to grab his cock through his pants. I was honestly impressed with the level of detail I was achieving, given how much I sucked at decorating cookies. Maybe kid-friendly cookies weren't my thing, but adult-version cookies were.

"Is that his…" Sunny's voice trailed off as she looked over my shoulder to see my cookie, her breasts brushing against my arm in the process.

"It is."

"Oh my. Santa sure does have a package to deliver," she teased, pulling her lower lip in between her teeth.

I leaned over to look at her Mrs. Claus cookie and swallowed hard when I realized that Sunny had created the illusion of crotchless panties.

"That's it," I growled, dropping everything and pushing

away from the island. Her head whipped up as she looked at me with confusion.

"What's wrong?"

"Nothing your tight pussy can't fix," I said as I gently grabbed her, threw her over my shoulder, and carried her down the hallway to our bedroom, making sure not to put too much pressure on her stomach.

I carefully dropped her to the bed and began stripping my clothes off as Sunny watched, still chewing her lower lip. She knew how much it turned me on and did it on purpose.

Once all of my clothes were off, I climbed onto the bed and worked on removing hers as I placed kisses all over her body.

I grabbed the candy cane vibrator from the nightstand and turned it on, slowly rubbing it along her nipples as I slid my fingers along her slit, covering them with her arousal. She closed her eyes and arched her back as her legs fell open, inviting me in. I slid a finger inside, then quickly inserted another, loving how tight her pussy gripped them.

She moaned and gripped the sheets beneath her as I pulled my fingers out and inserted the long stick part of the vibrator inside of her, lining it up so the curve of the candy cane hit her clit. I knew it would only take seconds for her to come, especially with how intense the vibration on this toy was.

"Fuck!" she cried, gripping harder as she came.

I chuckled and slowly pulled the toy out, turning it off and tossing it to the side. My dick was hard and desperate to be inside of her as I slowly climbed on top and lined myself up at her entrance.

"Don't tease me," she whispered, her eyes fluttering open. "I might have come once, but I'm not done for the night. Fuck me hard, how I like it."

I pushed inside, loving the way she hissed and squirmed beneath me as she tried to get me in deeper. Fucking Sunny was my favorite thing to do, and I planned to spend the entire night doing just that.

Blame It On The Candy Canes
<u>Five</u>
Andi

"We're going to be late," I warned as Zach stayed perched between my legs as I sat on the cold metal island in the middle of Sugarplum Sweets. "We were just supposed to grab extra supplies and head straight to Frosty Fest."

"Yeah, and I wanted to eat you out before we're stuck there, being busy all day. It's the stress reliever we both need. Now stop complaining, and let me get you off."

I closed my eyes, thankful that no one would be coming in this morning because all of the staff that was working the booth were already at Frosty Fest getting it set up. I had offered to come grab any extra inventory that we had when we saw how large the crowd was at the parade. Even with planning for extra traffic this year, I didn't seem to account for how much extra there really was.

Zach sucked my clit, gripping my thighs as he held me in place, forcing me to see stars as my pussy spasmed against his face.

"Oh my God!" I cried, grabbing a handful of his hair and pulling as my head fell back and a rush of air fell past my parted lips.

He slowly stood up and wiped the corners of his lips as a devilish smirk played on his lips.

"See, aren't you feeling a little more relaxed now?" he said, extending his hand to help me down.

"Yeah, but not as relaxed as I will be after you fuck me good and hard," I said, looking over my shoulder as I made no effort to pull my dress down after it had been gathered at my waist while he devoured me.

I planted my feet firmly and leaned forward, loving the cold air against my swollen clit. I heard his zipper as he freed his cock from his jeans and then slid inside me.

A lot had changed between us in two years like us moving in together and getting engaged. Not only that, he had become a co-owner of Sugarplum Sweets and now handled the online store that we had created to keep up with the demand from out-of-state visitors.

I gripped the edge of the island and held on as he pulled out and slammed inside me, doing it over and over, knowing how much I loved it. I could already feel another orgasm approaching as he purposely hit my G-spot.

He slipped his hand around the front and rubbed my clit while holding me steady with the other hand. It was going to be hard, fast, and dirty—just the way we liked it. As he pounded into me harder with every thrust, I felt the tingle along my spine as my orgasm climbed.

"Fuuuuccckkkk!" he growled, releasing his load as I spasmed around him.

I knew that we had a very long day ahead of us with Frosty Fest, but at least now we would both be a little more relaxed and ready to start on the right foot.

By the time we got there, the parade had just ended, and

everyone was making their way inside the mall where the festivities would take place. There was already a line at Sugarplum Sweets, wrapping around several corners, which instantly spiked my anxiety that we would run out of stock within the first five minutes.

"Don't worry. We've got this. It'll be fine," Zach assured me, squeezing my hand as we squeezed into the booth that was packed full of delicious treats.

I pulled my shoulders back and put on the *Master Baker* apron Zach had gotten me for Christmas the first year we were together. I loved it and found that it brought me good luck, so I insisted on wearing it today. Though, I did have to tell him he wasn't allowed to wear his in public since it had *Masturbater* on it.

"Did they let everyone in early?" I asked Liv, my assistant manager.

"Nope. They all rushed in and came straight here as soon as the doors opened. Autumn took charge of getting everyone situated before I could. We have three people talking to customers with each of them having an assistant to pull their orders. It's been pretty seamless so far, but then again, we've only been open for fifteen minutes."

"We're going to sell out in a matter of hours," I mumbled, my nerves already getting the best of me.

"It will be fine. Trust the process," Zach assured me, running his hand soothingly across my back.

I took a deep breath, nodded, and got to work.

<u>Six</u>

Zach

"We are sold out of the coconut truffles, but be sure to check online in a few days if you aren't able to make it to the store tomorrow. We have free shipping on orders of $25 or more," I said, handing a postcard to the lovely couple in front of me.

"Thank you. We come every year for the festival, but this year is busier than we've ever seen. We almost didn't get a hotel room," the older woman said, taking it. "But I'm happy to know that we can buy directly from you online. I'll have my granddaughter help me get it set up, but now I can have delicious treats year-round without having to wait for Frosty Fest."

I smiled and finished putting their items in the overly full bag. Not only had we run out of a few popular items like sugar cookies and truffles, but we were almost out of bags. Even with extra planning, we fell short this year with the heavy traffic no one seemed to expect.

Andi and I had spent almost the entire day cooped up in the booth, trying to get through as many customers as possible. There were several shift changes to allow everyone time to go shop and take a break, but Andi refused to leave.

"Alright, it has officially slowed down some," Liv said, putting her hand on Andi's shoulder. "You are done for the day. Go home."

"You can't kick me out," Andi said with a laugh, shaking her head.

The line had died down considerably, now with only about ten people instead of the fifty some that had continuously wrapped around the other booths for the last four hours.

"I can and I will. You've been here long enough. The line is manageable now. Go home and get some rest. I know you haven't slept in days. Plus, I'm sure Candy needs attention."

I chuckled as I watched Andi's cheeks flush with color.

"Our new puppy," I whispered in her ear, making sure Liv didn't hear me.

Before Andi and I started dating, I agreed to attend a Christmas party with her and pretend to be her boyfriend. That night, I won a candy cane-shaped vibrator that was appropriately named Candy. A few months ago at the shop, someone overheard me talking to Andi about Candy and asked who it was. I didn't know what to say and was on the spot, so I lied and told them we were getting a dog. Andi fell in love with the idea, and a few weeks ago, we brought home a beagle that we named Candy.

"Oh. Yes. Candy," Andi stammered. "Our puppy."

"You better get home before she chews through your couch again," Liv said with a soft laugh. "I've got this. Whatever we sell out of, I'll refer people to the online store if they don't want to check in tomorrow. Although I think most people like the idea of shopping online now, especially with the free shipping. It's giving a lot of them an excuse to buy $25 worth of junk food."

"Hey—we do not sell *junk food*," Andi countered, pointing her finger at Liv.

Liv rolled her eyes as she playfully swatted it away.

"You know what I mean. Now go. Get. We don't want you here anymore."

Andi pretended to pout as she took her apron off and stuffed it back into the tote bag she brought with her. We said goodbye to everyone as we snuck out of the booth and into the mall, where Frosty Fest was still very much happening.

"Did you want to go home or do some shopping first?" I asked, not knowing if she was too tired to do anything but sleep. She always overworked herself this time of year, and no matter how hard I tried, I couldn't stop her.

"We still need to get the ornaments for the exchange at your parent's house," she said, chewing her nail as she thought about it. "I need to get a few more things for my parents too. Plus a gift for Candy."

"Then let's do some shopping." I smiled and took her hand, letting her lead me wherever she wanted to go. It didn't matter to me what we did as long as I was with Andi.

Blame It On The Blizzard
<u>Seven</u>
Brynlee

"Do you think we brought enough books?" I asked Sebastian as I chewed my lower lip.

"This is all that they sent us, so unfortunately, it will have to be. I thought for sure five hundred would be plenty when I requested them, but I had no idea Frosty Fest would be this big this year."

"That's because *you guys* drew all of this attention to it by being New York Times bestselling authors who only do book signings at Frosty Fest," Hadley quipped, squeezing into the booth for Sugarplum Gifts, which just happened to be next to us this year.

"Well, it's hard to travel these days," I said with a sigh, rubbing my hand over my stomach.

"That's not a bad thing," Hadley agreed as she sat her stuff down. "The extra business in Sugarplum Falls has benefited everyone. Other than the insane line outside to get in, no one has complained."

"Are you sure you should be working the booth today?" I asked, concern etched on my face.

"I'll be fine. My doctor said that as long as I don't start

having contractions again, we should be good. I'll rest as often as I can, and we have a full staff working the booth today. I'm more of just a backup if they need it."

Hadley had met the love of her life when an out-of-towner stopped into Sugarplum Gifts, ready to ask for directions to the next town, but ended up asking for a date instead. Their love story was that of a whirlwind romance, with him proposing two months after they started dating. They got married right away, and Hadley found out she was pregnant a few months before I found out I was expecting our second child.

"You still need to take it easy," I warned, eying her bump suspiciously.

She had spent the past week going in to be monitored after having contractions off and on. She was already thirty-seven weeks pregnant, so the baby would be fine if he came early, but we all wanted him to cook a little longer if possible.

"You both need to take it easy," Sebastian countered, giving both of us a pointed look.

"That's what I keep saying," my aunt Beth said as she walked up to our table, holding Annie's hand.

"Hi, my baby," I cooed, getting up from my chair to go around the table to get her. "Mama missed you already." I picked her up and nuzzled her close to my face as she sat gently on my stomach.

"Miss Mama," Annie said, her little voice already sounding sleepy. It didn't surprise me any, given how early we had gotten her up to go to the Frosty Fest parade this morning.

"Looks like someone needs a nap soon," I commented softly, brushing a strand of hair out of her face.

"I'm going to head home so she can get a good nap. If she's up for it later, I'll bring her back, and we'll do some shopping." My aunt smiled, and I loved how much my family had rallied around me and Sebastian once I knew they existed. It was weird going almost my whole life thinking that I wasn't wanted, only to find out that I had an aunt and cousin who had been desperately trying to find me all those years.

"I don't think we'll be here the entire day," I said, cuddling my sweet girl a little longer. "With the line outside, I have a feeling we'll sell out early. We might stick around for an hour or so in case anyone comes and wants us to sign a copy of their book that they bring with them, but it doesn't make sense to sit here all day if we're out of books."

"I know that Brynlee wanted to do some shopping today, so I can always come by and pick up Annie once we're done here," Sebastian offered, rubbing a hand along Annie's back.

"We can play it by ear and see how everything goes," Beth said, reaching her arms out as I passed Annie to her.

We were down to the last few minutes before they opened the doors, and the madness ensued. I didn't want to say goodbye to my daughter, but I was also excited to share this moment with my husband. We started as strangers forced to share a cabin while riding out one of the worst storms Sugarplum Falls had ever seen, to becoming a married couple who cowrote bestselling novels together. It had been a wild and unpredictable ride, but I wouldn't change any of it.

<u>Eight</u>

Sebastian

"Looks like luck is on your side because you just got the very last copy," I said, smiling up at the older woman who was grinning from cheek to cheek as I signed her copy of the book after getting it from Brynlee, who had already signed it.

"My granddaughter is going to be so thrilled. She loves to read, and when I told her you guys were going to be here, I thought she was going to shit her pants."

My eyebrows rose as a grin tugged on my lips at her comment. If I had to guess, I would say she was in her seventies with gray curly hair and wrinkles that dotted her eyes and mouth, evidence of a life filled with happiness and laughter.

"Does your granddaughter live in town?" I asked as I closed the book and handed it to her.

"No, she's away at college in New York City. She wants to be a big-shot lawyer and never has time to visit. But now that I have this, she just might." She grinned a mischievous smile as she waved the book in her hand.

"Are you going to bribe her with it?"

"Yes. And I'm going to remind her that I'm not getting any younger, so if she wants to see her grandma before she dies, she better get her butt back to Sugarplum Falls before it's too late."

Brynlee covered her mouth and tried to hide the laughter.

"I won't keep you too long as you have a line wrapped around the corner," the woman said, looking over her shoulder. "But do you think I could bother both of you for a picture?"

"It would be our pleasure," Brynlee said, pushing away from the table and standing up.

We got in position, making sure the woman didn't trip over anything as she joined us for a quick selfie. I handed her phone back and thanked her for stopping by as I noticed Brynlee holding her back.

"Are you okay?" I asked, immediately concerned.

Brynlee was twenty-nine weeks pregnant and thankfully hadn't had any big issues with this pregnancy. With Annie, she'd started having decreased fetal movements in the last two weeks of her pregnancy and had to be induced.

"Yeah, just getting a little sore."

She smiled at the two younger women who approached our table, looking nervously at me as they held onto the books in their hands.

"You should take a break," I offered, worried about her.

"I'll be okay. We're officially out of books, so I can't imagine we'll stay too long."

I nodded and turned my attention to the two ladies waiting for me.

"Hello, how are you ladies doing today?" I asked, not sitting as I needed to stand and stretch my legs some.

"Good, thank you," one of them said before lowering her

eyes while a faint blush washed over her cheeks.

"We know that you guys are here for your new book, but we were hoping there might be a chance you would be willing to sign some of our F.E. Tish books," the other one explained, turning her books to face me.

"Sure. Not a problem at all." I grabbed my pen and took the books from them while the other girl looked nervously at Brynlee.

"I was hoping that you might sign mine for me as well," she said, stepping in front of Brynlee and sliding a tote bag off her arm before setting it on the table in front of her.

"Me?" Brynlee asked with pure confusion.

"Yeah. I've been reading your books for years, and I can't believe I finally get to meet you."

"Oh my gosh," Brynlee replied as I signed the last few books in front of me. "I would be honored."

I grinned at my wife as tears dotted the corners of her eyes, genuinely touched by this moment.

We continued to work for two straight hours, surprised by how many people showed up with copies of our books for us to sign. We talked and took pictures, the energy from those around us making ours skyrocket.

I always thought that I wanted a life hidden in the shadows where people didn't know who I was or the stories I created. But after meeting Brynlee, I realized that it was better to put myself out there and let people get to know the real person behind my pen name. Being surrounded by so many who loved the books Brynlee and I created—both separately and together—was a gift I never would get tired of.

Blame It On The Reindeer
<u>Nine</u>
Jasmin

"Alright, we are almost ready to rock and roll," I said, more to myself than to the noisy little elves who were already hyped up on sugar.

It was early—super early—and I was guessing that they had snuck into the marshmallows that were set out for the hot chocolate that was supposed to be for *after* the parade was over. But they were lively and energetic, so I couldn't complain about that.

But the problem was that they were so lively and energetic that they brought the noise level up so high I couldn't get anyone to hear me as I tried to get everyone's attention before we headed out to start the Frosty Fest parade.

"Attention," I shouted, still not able to get my voice above the loud decibels of the kids. I tossed my head back in frustration and was ready to try again when Brody placed his hand on my lower back to calm me.

"Santa is watching," he said, his voice booming through the room as the kids suddenly stopped talking and turned to face us.

He grinned and winked at me, taking a step back so I could have everyone's attention.

"It's that time," I said, smiling as the teens and adults came to join us now that they could hear me. "I want to go over a few things before we get started. First, safety is our number one priority. While we're all here to have fun, I need all of the elves on their best behavior today. That means *no* jumping off of the floats and no fighting. Each float has at least two adult elves, so be on your best behavior and listen to them.

"The parade will be the same as every year. The reindeer will start, and the Sugarplum Falls High School marching band will follow. After that, the floats are already lined up and ready to go. Each float will have a handful of elves that will be responsible for tossing candy canes into the crowd. Try to make sure you guys are spacing it out so we don't run out in the first five minutes. We have a much larger crowd than we've ever had before, so we really need to make sure to space them out as much as possible. Adult elves, it'll be your responsibility to monitor your supply and to make sure you have enough to get through the entire parade."

There were head nods and thumbs up as everyone collectively agreed to what I was asking. I took a deep breath as everyone scattered off, heading to where they needed to be.

"Thanks for your help," I said to Brody, turning to face him before having to rush off.

"My pleasure. Go kick butt with the parade." He leaned in and kissed the tip of my nose.

"Okay. I'll come check on you as soon as I can. Are you nervous?"

"About having my own booth at Frosty Fest? A little bit."

"Don't be," I assured him, hating that I felt so rushed right now. "You're going to do great. We don't have any other vendors this year with anything similar to what you have. You're going to kill it and probably sell out within minutes."

"I doubt that, but thank you."

"I'm serious, Brody. Those wood nativity scenes you made are beautiful, and the metal ornaments will go super fast. Not to mention the other non-Christmas stuff you have. You're going to be very popular today. I just know it."

"Thank you. Now get out there before the parade starts without you," he teased, smacking my ass as he turned and headed to the booth he needed to finish setting up.

I gave him a playful look over my shoulder, knowing that we would pick up where he left off later once we got back to the ranch.

When Brody first asked me to move in with him at the ranch, I was hesitant because my job was in Sugarplum Falls, and I didn't want to have to worry about commuting every day, especially during the winter. But once I moved in with him, I found that it was easy to do a lot of my work from home, outside of planning for Frosty Fest.

I headed outside, pulling my scarf tighter around my neck as the frigid cold nipped at my face. Even with temperatures well below freezing, the people of Sugarplum Falls still made it out to Frosty Fest, which just proved how much of a difference an event like this can have on an entire community. And I was the proud woman who was able to make all of it happen.

<u>Ten</u>

Brody

"Do you sell online?" an older man asked as he and his wife held onto several pieces of hand-carved wood decorations.

"No, sorry. I don't have any clue how to set any of that up," I replied with a genuine smile as I saw Jasmin slip into the booth beside me.

"I'll be helping him get one up before next year," she said proudly as she placed a hand on my shoulder.

"Perfect," the woman answered. "We would love to give these as gifts to our family next year. We've been trying to get our kids to come out and celebrate Christmas in Sugarplum Falls with us, but they always say they're too busy. After Paul took that nasty spill earlier in the year, they started coming around more often. I'm hopeful that we can get them out here next year."

"That would be wonderful," Jasmin replied. "I haven't seen the girls in so long. It would be great to have them back in Sugarplum Falls and meet their children."

"I'll let them know you said that." The woman nodded and wiped a stray tear from her eye.

I finished packing up their items and took the remaining ones they were holding onto.

"Do you guys need help getting these out to your car?" Jasmin asked, noticing how much they had purchased.

"Yes, please. If not, we can make a few trips," the man answered.

Jasmin pulled a walkie-talkie from her belt and spoke into it, asking a few of the junior elves to report to my booth for customer assistance.

I loved seeing her in her element and how easily she ran things at Frosty Fest. When she first told me about it, I thought the *Frozen Palooza* was a cheesy get-together for the Christmas-obsessed people of Sugarplum Falls. But after attending the first year I was here, my mind was quickly changed.

"Thank you again," I said, smiling at the couple as they walked away with their arms full and following the four teenagers who had come over to help them get everything to their car.

"Wow," Jasmin said, nodding as she looked around my booth. "You're almost sold out, and the day isn't even half done."

"I know. I think they took the majority of it," I teased, feeling my grin tug at my cheeks.

I was a bit iffy about whether or not to set up a booth at Frosty Fest, but after two years of Jasmin begging me to do it, I finally caved. It wasn't that I didn't want to do it last year; I just hadn't had the time to sit down and work on making stuff for it. It was wild to think that things I'd spent months on building just sold within a matter of minutes.

"Well, once you're completely sold out, I'll have someone come over to help you tear down your booth. Then you'll be free for the rest of the day."

"Thank you, but I don't need the help. I can get it."

"Why are you so difficult?" she asked, planting her hands on her hips and narrowing her eyes at me. Thankfully, I didn't have a line right now because I wanted to enjoy this moment with her without it being interrupted.

"You know better than to do that," I warned, my eyes roaming down her body.

"What are you going to do about it?" she pressed, fire in her eyes.

I reached forward and grabbed her, pulling her right into my chest.

"I'm going to take you home and fuck you so hard that your pussy needs three to five days to recover. I'm going to fill you so full of my cum that it will be dripping down your legs."

I felt her shudder against me as I gently rubbed my thumb over her cheek.

"Promises, promises," she said with a dramatic sigh.

"You better stop with that attitude, or I'm going to close my booth early and take you back to your office and fuck it out of you."

She smiled and shook her head, patting my chest before stepping away.

"You have customers, and I have elves to chase down. I'll come back and check on you in a bit," she said, waving at the couple that was looking at the metal ornaments on the table.

"I'll see you in a bit," I confirmed, already hating the empty feeling in my chest I got every time we were apart.

Thankfully, it was only a few more hours of working Frosty Fest, and then we would both be off until the New Year.

When I first met Jasmin, I couldn't believe my luck with the pain-in-the-ass woman who got herself stranded at my ranch in one of the worst snowstorms in Sugarplum Falls. Now I was looking forward to a white Christmas, cuddled up at the ranch with the woman I planned to ask to marry me on Christmas day.

Blame It On The Carols
<u>Eleven</u>
Makayla

"You know you can relax, right? You don't have to guard the bathroom," I said as Patrick stood rigidly by the door. "I'll just be a few minutes."

"It's all yours," Tony replied as he came out, making sure no one was hiding inside and waiting to attack me.

"Thank you." I smiled at my security team and ducked into the bathroom, closing the door behind me. My nerves were a wreck, but that's what happens when you decide to surprise your fiancé by ending your world tour early and coming home to surprise him for Christmas.

I needed a few minutes to get myself together after flying in late last night and getting back to town an hour ago. I didn't want anyone to know I was back yet, and aside from Jasmin, no one was expecting me at all. She and I had been in touch as she helped me set everything up to surprise Aiden by performing on one of the floats in the Frosty Fest parade this morning.

Tony brought me straight to the mall, and we snuck in before anyone else started arriving. Jasmin made sure I had everything I needed waiting for me in her office and even gave me access to a private bathroom where I could change and freshen up.

I looked in the mirror, hating the bags under my eyes from lack of sleep. The past few months had been busy with back-to-back concerts as I wrapped up my tour. I was supposed to go to Japan for my next stop, but my manager, Curtis, had some issues with the venue, and we had to pull out again. But I hadn't told Aiden that because Curtis had the genius idea to surprise him instead.

I applied my makeup and then slipped into the red sparkly gown that Jasmin had left for me. It had a lovely faux fur shawl to go with it, which would be nice given it was freezing balls outside and I was pretty sure I was going to die from the cold.

"How's it going? Do you have everything you need?" Jasmin asked from the other side of the door.

I smoothed my hands down the front of my dress and gave one final look in the mirror before opening the door.

"Oh my God, you look so beautiful," Jasmin said, covering her mouth with her hands as she smiled.

"Thank you. I don't know that there's enough makeup in the world to hide how exhausted I look, but I tried."

"You can't tell," she assured me. "I promise. Aiden is going to flip when he sees you."

"Do you think everyone is going to give it away before he does?"

"No, I purposely told him and Sam that they need to be at the front of the parade so he'll see you before the rest of the crowd does."

"Good thinking," I said, genuinely impressed with how much detail she had gone into to make this work for me.

"That's why they pay me the little bucks," she teased with a wink. "The kids are getting their elf costumes on as we speak, so if you want to hang out in here for a bit, I'll come get you right before we start."

"Sounds like a plan. Thanks for your help with setting all of this up."

"Thank *you* for performing in our parade. The crowd is going to go crazy over this, and in case you haven't noticed, it's bigger than ever this year."

"We're aware," Patrick said dryly, standing by the door with his arms locked in front of him.

I rolled my eyes, but deep down, I was thankful they were there with me. Patrick and Tony had been the best security detail I could ever wish for, and I was grateful that they uprooted their lives and moved to Sugarplum Falls two years ago when I decided to stay.

Even though it was a small town and it always felt safe to me, we had seen firsthand just how far an obsessed stalker would go with trying to find me. While I sometimes thought they were a little extra with how serious they were about things, I knew that I wasn't someone who could afford to let their guard down, especially now that I was coming back from being on tour for the last five months.

Jasmin left, closing the door behind her while I walked around her office, looking at the pictures on the walls. I didn't want to sit and risk messing up my dress, plus I was too nervous to be still. I needed to get some of this anxious energy out before I got up on a makeshift stage on the float and performed in front of everyone.

Half an hour later, Jasmin poked her head in to let me know that it was time. I hiked up my dress so I didn't trip over it and followed Tony out while Patrick fell in line behind me. Thankfully, everyone else was already gone, likely on their floats like Jasmin had said they would be. The goal was for me to come out right before it started so we could keep it a secret for as long as possible.

We walked outside, the cold air nipping at my skin as I accepted Tony's hand as he helped me onto the float and then guided me to the stage. People immediately began talking and pointing when they realized who I was, so I lifted my finger to my lips and asked them to keep my secret.

I took my place at the front of the float and gently blew into the microphone a few times to make sure it was on. There were six floats in front of me, which worked so I didn't have to compete with the high school marching band. My float had the cutest little elves lined up around the sides as Tony and Patrick stood off to the side, watching the crowd.

"It's showtime," Jasmin called out as she breezed past us, heading to the very front.

I took a deep breath in and slowly let it out, forcing all of my anxiety to go with it. In a very short time, I was going to see the love of my life and I couldn't wait to be reunited with Aiden.

Twelve

Aiden

"It's colder than balls out here," I grumbled, rubbing my hands together to try to stay warm.

"Stop complaining," Sam replied with a roll of his eyes. "It's Frosty Fest. It's always a good time, so try to enjoy it."

"I would enjoy it more if Mak were here," I said quietly, not that there was a single person in Sugarplum Falls who *didn't* know how much I missed her.

I hated that I was having to spend Christmas without her this year, but we both knew that this would happen when we decided to be together. She had uprooted her life in LA and moved to Sugarplum Falls to be with me, so I couldn't be upset that she was gone the past five months as she did her world tour. While I would have loved to go with her, I couldn't afford to take that much time off from work, and there was no way in hell that I would allow her to take care of me. It wasn't that I didn't respect Makayla or the money she made, but I was not the kind of guy who could sit back and allow someone else to pay for things for me. Plus, she was so busy with the tour that it wasn't like we would have much time to spend together anyway.

The parade started with the reindeer leading the way, followed by the marching band. I was trying to get myself in the holiday spirit and enjoy it, but I couldn't stop thinking about how much I wanted Makayla to be there with me. I tried to smile and wave as the first few floats passed by, then stopped when I heard a familiar voice.

My eyes immediately flew to the float where the sound was coming from, nearly bulging from my head when I saw my beautiful fiancée standing on the makeshift stage singing *I'll Be Home For Christmas*. I blinked a few times, making sure I wasn't hallucinating.

Sam nudged me with his elbow, but I couldn't pull my attention away from her. Her eyes locked with mine as she smiled and blew a kiss at me.

"Guess it's going to be a great Christmas after all," Sam said, clapping me on the back as I felt someone push their way to stand beside me.

"She sure does sound great up there, doesn't she?" Curtis, her manager, said as he smiled up at her as she passed by.

"How… Why… When…" I couldn't get the words out as so many questions raced through my mind.

"Makayla will explain everything," he said with a shrug and turned his attention back to the parade. "It really is such a fun event. I can see why she loves being here."

"They love having her here," I commented, nodding to the people who were screaming and jumping with excitement once they saw her. "And since no one—and I mean *no one* in town knew she would be here, it's a great surprise."

Curtis smirked, and I knew he was behind this whole thing. But that didn't matter right now. Nothing mattered. The love of my life was back, and as soon as the parade was over, I would have her in my arms again.

****

It was the longest thirty minutes of my life as I waited for Makayla to finish with the parade. I waited impatiently with Jasmin where all of the floats were taken to the back parking lot. I knew Makayla had Tony and Patrick with her because I had seen them frowning at the crowd as they stood beneath her on the float. But if I had to guess, there were at least a dozen other security guys here today.

Finally, she was done and I grinned when I saw her heading my way. She took off running, much to Tony and Patrick's dismay, and headed right for my arms.

I wanted to pick her up and never let go, but I also didn't want to ruin her dress by splitting the slit that already went up her thigh. She smiled as she rushed into my arms, letting me hold her as she wrapped hers around my neck.

"Merry Christmas!" she said happily as she brushed her lips against mine.

"Merry Christmas indeed," I replied, my body already responding to hers. "When did you get back? How did you get back? Why didn't you tell me?"

I still had a ton of questions, but I knew we would get to them in time.

"We should get you inside," Tony said sternly, leaning in so we could hear him.

"Okay," she replied with a nod as she pulled away. She reached down and held my hand as we followed Jasmin inside the mall through a back door and went straight to her office.

"My tour ended early," Makayla explained, looking up at me once we were inside and by ourselves. Tony had already cleared the office to make sure it was safe before giving us some privacy. "I flew back late last night and got in early this morning. We came straight here. Jasmin and I have been talking for a few weeks. I wanted to surprise you and she suggested having me perform in the parade."

"I was definitely surprised," I said, wanting to reach out and touch her as she shimmied out of her dress and let it fall to the floor.

"Sorry I didn't tell you sooner. Curtis came up with the idea, and I just ran with it. I hope you're not mad."

"I couldn't be mad at you if I tried, Mak."

"Well then, I guess the spanking I was hoping for isn't going to happen," she teased, standing before me in nothing but a black lace bra and matching panties.

"Your security detail is right outside the door," I said quietly, stepping toward her as my fingers itched to roam over her skin.

"And they know not to come in until I tell them to."

"What if they hear us?"

"I guess we're gonna have to be quiet."

My eyes roamed her body again as my dick strained against my jeans. I hadn't been able to touch her in months, and I wasn't about to wait any longer. Those late-night FaceTime calls did nothing to quell the ache I felt from wanting to be inside of her.

"I'm here to stay for a while," she assured me as she reached for my belt and undid it. "Let's do a quick fuck to get it out of our systems, then we can focus on taking our time when we get home later."

I pulled my lower lip in between my teeth and tried to suppress the growl that begged to come out. She turned and bent over the edge of the desk, her ass pointed up as she spread her legs.

"We don't have all day," she teased, playfully shaking her ass for me as she pulled her panties to the side and showed me her pussy.

I groaned and unzipped my jeans, pulling my cock free as I stood behind her and lined myself up at her entrance. I reached down and swiped a finger along her folds, loving that she was already wet for me.

"Fuck, baby," I moaned, sliding my finger inside of her and spreading her arousal along her lips. "I missed this pussy."

"She missed you too. Now stop talking and fuck me before I explode."

I chuckled and removed my finger as I slid my cock inside of her and held onto her hips. Her panties were pulled to the side, but knowing she was still wearing them as I fucked her without a condom was such a turn-on that I struggled not to come right away.

I gripped her hips and held on as I slammed into her, knowing how much she loved it. She reached down between her legs, rubbing her clit as I fucked her hard and deep. Neither of us was going to last long right now, but that didn't matter because she was home and we now had all the time in the world to get our fill of each other.

She arched her back and squeezed her thighs as she spasmed around me, bringing herself to climax. While I would have loved to do that for her, I knew that I would get her off later when we didn't have to rush. I felt my balls tighten as I thrust harder, releasing my load inside of her.

My head tipped back as I tried to catch my breath, not ready to pull out of her just yet.

"Fuck I missed that," she panted, looking at me over her shoulder.

"Me too, baby."

I knew people were going to start to wonder what was taking us so long, so I pulled out and grabbed a few tissues for us to clean up with. She got dressed, and I was happy to see she had brought comfortable clothes to change into. Not only that, she looked adorable in her Sugar Faced Bar hoodie and leggings that she would likely freeze her ass off in the second she stepped outside. But at least I was there to keep her warm however I could.

Once she was done, I helped her hang the dress after it was slipped back into the garment bag. She grabbed a duffle bag from the floor and tossed it over her shoulder before I grabbed it and put it over mine. She might have been used to doing things on her own while on tour, but she was back in town now, and I was going to take care of her every chance I got.

"So, did you want to go home right away or do some shopping?" I offered, secretly hoping she would say go home so we could get straight to round two.

"Shopping," she replied, giving me a cheeky grin. "I know

you want to go home so we can pick up where we left off, but I haven't done *any* of my Christmas shopping, so I need to do that while I'm here."

"Okay, fine," I groaned playfully, letting my head fall forward in disappointment.

She wrapped her hands around my bicep and gently squeezed as she smiled up at me.

"I can ask Sam if he'll make you a peppermint mocha latte if that makes you feel better?" she teased, batting her eyes.

"You think you're cute, don't you?" I asked, narrowing my eyes at her.

It was a running joke between us after Sam failed miserably at trying to play matchmaker between us when Makayla first came back to help her mom with the caroling competition. He knew I only drank black coffee, yet he sent her with a peppermint latte and two candy canes—Sam's idea of fixing every problem a couple could have.

"The cutest," she replied, batting her eyes.

I tickled her sides as we headed to the door and opened it. Tony and Patrick both looked away, refusing to make eye contact with either of us. The blush on her cheeks confirmed that she knew they knew what we had been doing.

Blame It On The Lattes
Thirteen

Avery

"I can't believe you're not working Frosty Fest this year," I said to Sam as we walked side by side with Kennedy in front of us, pushing the stroller.

"Family comes first," he replied as he squeezed my hand. "There's more to life than just lattes."

"Yes, but *you* are the king latte maker in Sugarplum Falls. People come from all over to get a latte from you."

"True, but today, they come from all over the world to be at Frosty Fest. My team is more than capable of handling today without me having to be there. Besides, I would much rather spend my time with my four beautiful ladies."

I smiled up at him as Kennedy came to a stop right in front of the food court.

"I'm hungry. Can we please get some lunch?"

"Absolutely. I'm hungry too," I said, smiling down at my little girl, who was growing up so quickly.

"Do you know what you want?" Sam asked, looking down at her.

"Pizza and breadsticks. The really long ones," Kennedy replied with a giggle.

"What about you?" He turned his focus to me, and for a moment, I got lost in his eyes.

It was hard to believe that this was my life now. Living in a small town that was overly obsessed with Christmas, married to the man of my dreams, and a mother to three beautiful girls. When Kennedy told us she had a dream about me having Sam's baby a while back, she kinda failed to mention it would be twins.

"I'll take a slice of pizza, please."

"Your usual?"

I nodded, loving that he learned all of our favorites early on and never forgot.

"Cool. I'll take Kennedy with me to get food if you want to take the twins and find us a table."

"Will do." I waved bye to Kennedy as she reached for Sam's hand, ready to get her food. The mall was packed with an outrageous number of people this year, so finding a table for all of us and the stroller was going to be tricky.

I pushed my way through the crowded tables and finally spotted one toward the back. I made a beeline for it, thankful that it was close to a wall where I could squeeze the stroller in. The girls were still asleep, which I was grateful for because trying to deal with fussy one-year-olds in a crowded mall was not my idea of fun. I pulled out the pack of wipes from the diaper bag and wiped down the table while I waited for them to get the food.

"Sorry it took so long. The line was huge," Sam said when he returned with Kennedy.

She sat directly across from me and immediately started eating her pizza as if she hadn't eaten in days. I teased her that she had a school stomach and an at home stomach, and they were far from the same. At school she didn't eat much and was more concerned with playing at recess, whereas at home, she ate like she was a fifteen-year-old boy right after football practice.

"I appreciate you getting us lunch. Thank you."

"My pleasure," he said before lifting the pizza to his lips and taking a bite. "I ran into Cassidy in the food court. She said to let you know that she got the rest of the stuff that was on your list."

"She's such a godsend," I replied, wiping the sauce from the corner of my mouth. It was great being close to my best friend, but even better that she worked at the largest store in Sugarplum Falls and was able to get her hands on a few toys I desperately wanted for the girls.

"Don't tell her that. It'll go to her head," Sam teased.

"Hey, I'll tell her whatever she wants to hear. She offered to watch the girls tonight and have a slumber party."

"Eh, she'll be fine. Plus, Kennedy is such a great big sister. She'll help Aunt Cassidy out if she needs it."

Kennedy didn't bother to stop eating so she could respond and instead gave us a thumbs up.

"True, but soon enough, Ginger and Noelle will be running all over, and they'll need even more help keeping an eye on those two."

When Sam and I first found out that we were expecting twin girls, we had the hardest time coming up with names that we loved. It seemed that everything we picked just didn't feel right. I threw Ginger in the mix because of my love for his gingerbread lattes, but I never thought he would go for it. It turned out that both he and Kennedy adored the name, so it was a winner.

With Noelle, we couldn't figure out what we wanted her name to be, and then one night, we were watching a Christmas special on TV, and Makayla Rhodes sang a chill-inducing version of *The First Noel*, and she started moving wildly in my stomach. We all agreed that she should be named our sweet Noelle.

Having twins had definitely kept Sam and me on our toes, especially with me still teaching at Sugarplum Falls Elementary School. But, like with all things, we learned to roll with the punches and appreciate the blessings life continued to give us.

Fourteen

Sam

"Ho, ho, ho," I said with my best Santa impression as Avery walked through the kitchen, looking for something.

"Who are you calling a ho?"

"No one. I'm pretending to be Santa so you can come sit on my lap and tell me what you want for Christmas."

"The last time I did that, we ended up conceiving twins," she teased, pointing a finger at me. "Besides, we don't have time for that. We have two closets full of presents that we need to get wrapped while we're kid-free."

I got up from the chair I was sitting on in the living room and stopped her by the island before she could gather more supplies.

"We have plenty of time to get the presents wrapped," I assured her, lifting her chin with my finger so she would be forced to look at me. "What we don't get plenty of time for is alone time. Just you and me."

"I know," she said with a heavy sigh. "I want that too, but I'm not going to be able to focus on anything else until this is done. It'll just sit there, weighing on my mind."

"Fine. But I'm making us some coffee."

Avery pulled back and looked past me to see the clock on the stove.

"It's already after eight."

"Yeah, and I have plans for you tonight, so I don't want to worry about either of us saying *I'm too tired, let's do it in the morning*," I said in my whiniest voice.

"I don't sound like that." Avery poked her finger hard into my chest.

"No, but you can't honestly tell me that the past few times we've had time to ourselves, we haven't both been too tired to enjoy it."

"True…"

"I know that we have a lot to get done with the presents," I assured her. "I'm not dismissing how you feel about it. It's a priority for me, too. But right now, I want nothing more than to make love to my wife in my own house where she can scream as loud as she wants to, and we don't have to rush it because one of the kids might wake up. Hell, we can even do it right here in the kitchen if we want to. The sky is the limit tonight, Avery. Let's not waste the gift of time we've been given."

"Oh my gosh, you're laying it on pretty thick tonight," she teased with an arched eyebrow.

"I'm just a man who knows what I want." I shrugged but noticed the humor dancing in her eyes.

"And I'm just a woman who only drinks properly made lattes. Don't come at me with any of that cheap coffee crap that Cassidy used to give me. If we're doing this, we're going all in."

"Fine. I'll get the lattes started while you gather the

wrapping supplies. I'll even raise the stakes and turn it into a *friendly competition.*"

"Why do you say it like that?" She narrowed her eyes and folded her arms over her chest.

"What? I'm just saying we can have a *friendly competition.*"

"Oh my God," she quipped, finally realizing what I was up to. "You're seriously going to turn this into strip wrapping again?"

"It worked so well for the twin's birthdays. Why not do it now? Unless you're afraid to lose?"

"I'm not afraid of anything," she said sternly, taking a step and invading my space. "Be prepared to go down."

"I'm more than prepared to go down on you, Avery. I'll go down on you right here, right now."

Her cheeks flushed with color as she realized what she said.

She scrunched her face and shook her head as she walked off, leaving me in the kitchen to start the lattes.

Once they were ready, I took them and joined her in the living room, where she was finishing separating the gifts into piles for each of the three girls, as well as separate piles for my family with gifts we still needed to wrap.

There were two rolls of wrapping paper, a pair of scissors, and several rolls of tape waiting for me on my side of the floor while Avery had her supplies set up the way she wanted them. In between us was a giant bag of peel-and-stick bows that I wasn't sure we needed, but Avery insisted on buying earlier when we popped into Waldon's for a few things.

"Alright, the piles are set and organized," she said after taking a sip of her latte and setting it on the coffee table. "The first one to finish five presents wins and the loser has to take off a piece of clothing. We'll go every five gifts finished until we reach the end."

"It's on." I rubbed my hands together and gave her my best seductive smile, which must have worked because she quickly looked away and crossed her legs.

I turned on some Christmas music to help set the tone and grabbed the first thing I could reach while Avery was already almost done wrapping hers. I forgot how quick she was and how she was used to doing this in a hurry when Kennedy was little.

By the time I finished wrapping my first gift, Avery tossed a small package into her pile of finished gifts.

"That's number five," she said with a flirtatious grin. "Strip."

"Calm down, it's one article of clothing," I teased as I pulled my sweater over my head and tossed it behind me.

"That's cheating."

"How so?"

"Because you're wearing more layers than me."

"Hey, I didn't make the rules." I held my hands in front of me as she pinned me with a look. "Fine." I grabbed the back of my shirt and pulled it off, noticing the way she watched me.

"That's better," she said with a grin.

"Well, enjoy the view while you lose 'cause I'm taking you down this time," I warned, grabbing a few presents at a time.

Her eyebrows pinched in confusion as she watched me line all three up on a piece of wrapping paper without cutting it to fit each one. I was a man on a mission and didn't have time to waste right now. I grabbed a piece of tape and secured it before cutting the paper from the rest of the roll.

"You do realize those are three separate presents, right?"

"Yep. Shouldn't you be worried about catching up instead of worrying about what I'm doing?"

She sighed heavily and rolled her eyes before grabbing a present to wrap.

Needing to win this round, I sat up on my knees and worked quickly to make two cuts to separate the paper where I needed, then quickly taped up all the sides. It was pure luck that I happened to grab the three boxes that had matching gifts for the girls, otherwise my little trick wouldn't have worked if they were all different sizes.

I slapped a bow on each one after adding a name label and moved them to the side while I grabbed another one to wrap. Avery was already working on her second present when I finished my fourth one.

"You better hurry up, or you're gonna get cold," I said, watching the way she looked at me.

She finished hers at the same time I grabbed my fifth one. Thankfully, it was a dress that was already in a gift box, so it was super easy to wrap. I found too much satisfaction in the sound of the scissors slicing through the paper as I cut exactly what I needed. A few pieces of tape and I was done.

"Alright, you lose this round," I declared, sitting back on my heels as I watched frustration cross my wife's face. "Take something off."

She had already gotten comfortable when we got home, which meant she likely wasn't wearing a bra under the hoodie she'd stolen from my side of the closet. She also didn't have any shoes or socks on, which eliminated those as easy things for her to remove.

"Fine, you win," she said sarcastically with a devious smile on her lips. She reached for the waistband on her yoga pants and pulled them painfully slow down her legs. I couldn't see much other than her long, beautiful legs, but I was confident I would win the next round as well.

"Happy?" she asked, batting her eyes.

I reached down and grabbed my erection through the fabric of my joggers, loving the way her eyes immediately followed.

"What do you think?"

"I think you better be careful, or you're going to lose this next round."

She reached over and stole five small gifts from the piles before I could. We both knew it wouldn't take any time for her to wrap those. Instead of trying to jump in and beat her since I already knew she would win this round, I did the most logical thing I could think of.

I pulled down my joggers, allowing my dick to spring free as it jutted up to my stomach. She stopped what she was doing and watched as I grabbed one of the bows, peeled off the paper, and stuck it to the tip of my cock.

"What are you doing?" she asked, her voice a tad bit squeakier.

"Accepting my loss on this round and wrapping your gift. Do you like it?" I stepped closer so my cock was almost lined up with her face.

"I love it. It's the perfect size and everything," she teased as she let the present she was trying to wrap fall to the floor. Her fingers wrapped around me, stroking slowly while she licked her lips.

"Well, lucky for us, it's the gift that keeps on giving."

I closed my eyes and let out a long, slow hiss as she pulled me into her mouth and began sucking. Avery knew exactly how to work me, which was unsettling because I no longer controlled whether I came in her mouth or if I got to come inside of her. She wore the pants in our relationship in almost every sense, and she had gotten very comfortable telling me exactly what she wanted in the bedroom. I had no idea what I did to get so lucky, but I wasn't complaining.

She continued to suck while using her hands to stroke the portion that didn't fit in her mouth, even though she had taken me all the way to the back of her throat.

"I don't want to come in your mouth," I warned, gently stroking her head.

She pulled back, letting me pop out of her mouth as she looked up at me with beautiful brown eyes.

"I want to come on your cock," she said, taking my hand as I helped her off of the floor. "Maybe in front of the Christmas tree?"

"I can make that happen." I led her over to the chaise part of the couch we had recently bought and sat down before helping her climb on top of me. "Turn around so you can see the tree."

She did as I asked, getting herself into reverse cowgirl position before lowering onto my cock. I gripped her hips and closed my eyes as I waited for her to adjust to my size. Two years together and it was still something we had to do because I never wanted to hurt her. Once she was situated, she leaned forward and started grinding against me, lining herself up so my dick rubbed her clit.

We had tried this position several times and she always loved it because of how easily she could get herself off without me touching her. It also allowed me to go deeper as she controlled the rhythm and pace.

I held onto her hips, loving that she hadn't bothered to wear panties either. We both knew that we would end up spending the majority of our night enjoying adult time with each other since it was so hard to come by these days.

She leaned forward, shifting her position slightly as I felt her pussy start to spasm around me. It was so hot that she used my cock to get herself off that I immediately followed, releasing my load deep inside of her.

A few minutes later, she glanced over her shoulder and gave me a sly smile as if she had planned this all along.

Blame It On The Secret Santa
<u>Fifteen</u>
Sean

"Hi, Santa," I said, lifting Lily's hands as I held her in my arms. She was way too little to care about him, given that she was only three months old, but it was still nice to start this tradition with her. Over the past two years, a lot of new traditions started after my brother Declan and his family moved back to Sugarplum Falls.

My father still had his ups and downs with his health as his dementia progressed, but we were all thankful for the time we had with him. When Cassidy and I found out we were having a baby, my father's face lit up with joy, and I was thankful we were blessed with him having a good day where he was able to process the news and celebrate with us.

"We're going to take the girls over to the reindeer pen when this is over. Do you want to go with us and show Lily?" Declan asked, standing beside me as his twin girls stood in front of us. It was hard to believe they were already six and in first grade, but it had been wonderful watching them grow up and be part of their lives.

"Do you think it's too cold out for her?" I asked, not having any idea whether the layers we'd put her in this morning were enough.

"I think she'll be okay," Cassidy said, squeezing her little baby feet and smacking her lips at Lily.

It was incredible just how much Lily looked like her mother.

"Then I guess we're going to check out the reindeer," I said as I playfully bounced Lily while holding her against my chest.

Once the parade was over, the majority of the crowd headed into the mall to start their shopping while those of us with kids went to the reindeer pen. It was fun seeing how much joy it brought the kids as their faces lit up seeing real reindeer.

I held Lily's hand out to try to pet the reindeer, but once it stuck its tongue out and tried to lick her, she got scared and started crying. I knew it was getting close to when she usually went down for a nap and was probably just tired.

"Aww, baby girl," Cassidy said, extending her arms to take her as Lily reached for her momma. "Are you sleepy?"

"It is about that time," I commented, watching how Lily instantly calmed once she was with Cassidy. "We can head inside if you want to try to get her down."

"I think that's a good idea. Then we can do some shopping while she sleeps."

"She definitely has a comfy place to do so," Declan said, nodding to the deluxe stroller we had with us.

"Hey, you gotta get the best of the best," I joked, even though it was technically true.

"That and it helps that we get a super sweet discount working at Waldon's," Cassidy added with a laugh. "We wouldn't have been able to afford it otherwise."

It really was a nice stroller with plenty of storage and lots of padding to keep her comfortable.

We headed inside, and I was surprised by how busy it was. There were people everywhere, and nearly every vendor that was set up had super long lines. A lot had changed in Sugarplum Falls over the past few years, which drove a lot of tourists to come see the adorable, Christmas-obsessed town.

Cassidy found a bench in a somewhat quiet part of the mall and sat down to nurse Lily while I headed for Sugarplum Lattes. I knew she would want a latte, and this way I could get it for her without her having to wait forever in line, even though it was moving surprisingly fast.

"Hey, how's it going?" Sam asked, nodding at me from the back of the booth as I approached the front of the line.

"Good. Cass is working on getting Lily down for her morning nap, so I thought I would grab her a latte. I thought you weren't working today?"

"I'm not. I just popped in for a moment to grab a few things."

I smiled and stepped forward to place our order. Sam waved as he ducked out the back and went on his way. I was sure we would run into him at some point, but then again, with the way the crowd looked at the moment, I wasn't so sure.

I grabbed our drinks and then carefully made my way back to the bench where Cassidy was sitting, careful not to spill them. I knew from experience that she wasn't the quick-to-forgive type, though this was a lot different than some stupid rumor that broke us up in high school. But still, Cassidy didn't play around when it came to her coffee.

"She's out," Cassidy said with a smile as she discreetly covered herself and shifted Lily to her shoulder before putting her in the stroller. There were plenty of blankets, just in case we needed them, but thankfully, it was warm enough in the mall that Lily should sleep peacefully. She was one of those babies who slept better with more noise and woke easily if it was too quiet.

"You ready to do some shopping?" I asked, handing her the latte as I set mine in the cup holder and pushed the stroller.

"I'm so ready. But you can't hang around when I'm shopping for your gift."

"Why not?"

"Because it wouldn't be very *Secret Santa* if you knew what I was getting you."

"What do you think the odds are that we would draw each other again?"

"I don't know. I kinda feel like Bruce had something to do with that. I can't prove it, but something tells me that the Waldon's Secret Santa gift exchange might be rigged," she teased, even though we both knew it wasn't. It was funny, though, that we had both drawn each other's names again this year. Thankfully, she didn't have to look up *what to give someone you hate for Christmas* this time. Or at least I hoped not…

<u>Sixteen</u>

Cassidy

"One day, the children all got a letter in the mail inviting them to the Christmas Cabin," I said, my voice barely above a whisper.

"Is she out?" Sean asked, leaning against the doorframe as he gazed adoringly at his baby girl in my arms.

"Yeah. She fell asleep early on in the story." I laughed softly. "I think those few minutes she was awake at Frosty Fest really wore her out."

He grinned, and I felt butterflies flutter in my stomach.

"Why don't I put her in her crib, and you can finish reading the story to me by the tree?"

"We don't have to do that. I've read it to everyone in this house at least twenty times. I'm sure even Max is tired of hearing it, and he usually loves everything about me."

"I don't know. I think as long as he got to curl up beside you and sleep, he wouldn't care what you did."

I nodded my head and grinned, knowing how much truth there was in that statement.

Max was the neediest dog I had ever met, but I still fell madly in love with the adorable, loving Doberman pinscher. He was one of the best dogs I had ever met, and he was the one who found out I was pregnant with Lily before anyone else knew. He was obsessed with laying his head on my stomach and constantly whimpered to get closer. A few weeks later, I realized I was more than just a few weeks late getting my period and wasn't surprised by the positive pregnancy test.

I handed Sean the book while I carefully stood up and put Lily in her crib. It was crazy to believe that we had a three-month-old baby girl and how quickly our lives had changed once she was born. We knew things would be different for a while, but neither of us was prepared for just how hard those sleepless nights would be.

Sean closed the door behind us as we quietly left her room and went to the living room. The baby monitor was already turned on and sitting on the coffee table with Max lying right next to it. He was overly protective of Lily and always had to be as close to her as possible.

We sat on the couch and I leaned against his chest as he wrapped his arms around me and held me tight. Cuddling was our favorite thing to do, especially on nights like tonight when we were both too tired to do anything.

"Did you remember to get the baby doll I asked for at Waldon's?" I asked, tilting my chin up slightly to see him.

"Nope. There is no talk about that stuff right now. I just want to sit and relax with you. But yes, I got it. And it's already wrapped and under the tree."

"Sorry," I said with a heavy sigh, letting myself relax against him. "Thank you for taking care of that."

"Not a problem."

It was weird to feel so connected to someone and to allow my walls to come down enough to allow him to help me with stuff. We'd grown a lot in the past two years, and all for the better.

I spent twelve years hating him for something he never did, and now I was going to spend the rest of my life loving him for all of the little things he did for me and Lily.

✱✱✱✱✱✱✱✱✱✱✱✱✱✱✱✱✱✱✱✱✱✱✱✱✱✱✱✱✱✱✱✱✱

Thank you for loving the Sugarplum Falls series so much that you wanted more. I truly enjoyed writing these bonus epilogues, and while I'm sad to be leaving this world that I so lovingly created, I'm excited to see where my creativity goes next. Thank you for being here and for loving these characters as much as I do!

If you're looking for more holiday stories, be sure to check out some of my standalone novellas!

If you'd like to chat and hang out, you can find me in my reader group on Facebook. We'd love to have you there! https://www.facebook.com/groups/2945710968775398/

Other Books By Samantha Baca

The Haven Brook Series
(small-town romantic suspense):

'Til Death Do Us Part (Haven Brook Book 1)

https://books2read.com/u/m2RJNR

The Cradle Will Fall (Haven Brook Book 2)

https://books2read.com/u/b6O0QE

The Ties That Bind (Haven Brook Book 3)

https://books2read.com/u/mqgoz8

A Very Haven Christmas (Haven Brook Book 4- Novella)

https://books2read.com/u/mvqGjj

Three Strikes, You're Gone (Haven Brook Book 5)

https://books2read.com/u/mvqL2z

The Dark Shadows Trilogy
(romantic suspense)

Five Steps Ahead (Dark Shadows Book 1)

https://books2read.com/u/38Q0gO

Ten Seconds Too Late (Dark Shadows Book 2)

https://books2read.com/u/3JRgVB

Against The Clock (Dark Shadows Book 3)

https://books2read.com/u/m2YwoR

The Stone Creek Series
(small town novellas)

Chocolate Covered Mistletoe (Stone Creek Book 1)

https://books2read.com/u/3LRk9N

Candy Coated Promises (Stone Creek Book 2)

https://books2read.com/u/mldP5Y

Pumpkin Spiced Possibilities (Stone Creek Book 3)

https://books2read.com/u/bojdwV

<u>Beaumont Creek Series</u>
<u>(small town)</u>

Just One Time (Beaumont Creek Book 1)

https://books2read.com/u/3G52zK

Second Chances (Beaumont Creek Book 2)

https://books2read.com/u/4Aj6Z0

Third Time's The Charm (Beaumont Creek Book 3)

https://books2read.com/u/b5lEyG

Four-ever Single (Beaumont Creek Book 4)

https://books2read.com/u/4j5jMX

Fifth Wheel (Beaumont Creek Book 5)

https://books2read.com/u/4XwKwa

Whiskey Mountain Series
(small town novellas)

Something To Talk About

https://books2read.com/u/4X62ag

Something To Think About

https://books2read.com/u/3GWAan

Something To Believe In

https://books2read.com/u/3yVzgB

Something To Live For

https://books2read.com/u/mllEOP

Sugarplum Falls Series
(holiday novellas - can be read as standalone)

Blame It On The Mistletoe
https://books2read.com/u/bw1rqe

Blame It On The Eggnog
https://books2read.com/u/38PPY6

Blame It On The Candy Canes
https://books2read.com/u/31DNo7

Blame It On The Blizzard
https://books2read.com/u/b6z6XE

Blame It On The Reindeer
https://books2read.com/u/baLAG6

Blame It On The Carols
https://books2read.com/u/me8E9z

Blame It On The Lattes
https://books2read.com/u/mB1E2A

Blame It On The Secret Santa
https://books2read.com/u/mY9dGY

Standalone Books

One Last Wish

https://books2read.com/u/mqg7D9

Finding Love In Apartment 2C (novella)

https://books2read.com/u/bze9aZ

Cocky Counsel: A Hero Club Novel

https://books2read.com/u/31Kzkn

All Is Fair In Food And War (novella)

https://books2read.com/u/bp8qjX

Holiday Books
(novellas)

Snow Place To Go

https://books2read.com/u/4A560N

A Very Merry Kissmas

https://books2read.com/u/bPDgy7

A Christmas Wish

https://books2read.com/u/4EKXpE

Holiday Hijinks

https://books2read.com/u/4DP6Ze

About the Author

Samantha lives in the southwest with her husband and two small children after abandoning her childhood dream of living in a cabin in Colorado when she found that she couldn't afford to live there and was deathly allergic to the woods. When she's not writing, she's usually spouting off sarcastic remarks while drinking wine out of a coffee mug to look like a functional adult while chasing down her toddlers. She enjoys spending time with her family, watching reruns of Friends, and the 24/7 flow of coffee that can be found in her veins. Be sure to follow her on social media for updates on what she's working on.

You can find her here:

Facebook:

https://www.facebook.com/AuthorSamanthaBaca

Instagram:

https://instagram.com/author_samantha_baca

Goodreads:

http://www.goodreads.com/authorsamanthabaca

Facebook Reader Group:

https://www.facebook.com/groups/2945710968775398/

Webpage:

www.samanthabaca.com

www.ingramcontent.com/pod-product-compliance
Lightning Source LLC
Chambersburg PA
CBHW030944310726
48969CB00008B/2377